Statues Across America

by Ann Shepard

⭐ Strategy Focus

As you read, think of **questions** to ask about different kinds of statues.

HOUGHTON MIFFLIN   BOSTON

Key Vocabulary

giant a huge, strong creature in folktales and stories

mysterious very hard to explain or understand

pedestal something that holds up a statue

square an open area in the center of a town or city

statue an image of someone or something, usually made of stone or metal

weakling a name for a person who is not strong

Word Teaser

What tiny animal lives inside the word **giant**?

Is there a statue in your town or city? Many
places in the United States have statues.

In New York City, you can see a
statue of a dog named Balto.

The real Balto ran a long way to bring
medicine to sick children.

This statue shows Paul Bunyan.
Paul Bunyan is a giant from a folktale.

Paul was very strong. He could dig holes
as big as lakes. Paul was not a weakling!

Many statues show real people. W. C. Handy played the trumpet. He helped invent a new kind of music. It was called "the Blues."

Sadako was a girl from Japan. She wanted to bring peace to the world.

One statue even honors seagulls! The
seagulls ate crickets that were eating crops.

The seagull statue is in a city square in Salt Lake City, Utah.

In a book called *Make Way for Ducklings*,
a family of ducks lives in the city of Boston.
There are statues of the ducks in a park there.

The ducks' backs are very shiny. Why?
There's nothing mysterious about this. Children
like to sit on the statues.

What statues can you see in your town or city?

NOTE

Putting Words to Work

1. Complete this sentence:
   A **weakling** cannot _____.

2. Why do you think a **statue** is sometimes put on a **pedestal**?

3. What question would you like to ask a **giant**?

4. Write directions for a classmate telling how to draw a **square**.

5. **PARTNER ACTIVITY:** Choose a word you learned in the book. Explain its meaning to your partner and give an example.

Answer to Word Teaser
An **ant**